ADVENTURES IN LITERATURE

NOVEL STUDY GUIDE

The Time Machine
H. G. Wells

HBJ Harcourt Brace Jovanovich, Publishers
Orlando   San Diego   Chicago   Dallas

Copyright © 1990 by Harcourt Brace Jovanovich, Inc.

All rights reserved. No part of this publication may be reproduced or transmitted in any form or by any means, electronic or mechanical, including photocopy, recording, or any information storage and retrieval system, without permission in writing from the publisher.

Requests for permission to make copies of any part of the work should be mailed to: Copyrights and Permissions Department, Harcourt Brace Jovanovich, Publishers, Orlando, Florida 32887.

Printed in the United States of America

ISBN 0-15-348525-6

CONTENTS

To the Student v
Introduction to *The Time Machine* 1
Chapter Cluster Worksheets
    Chapters I–II
        Reading Log 5
        Reading Check: Recalling the Facts 6
        Study Guide: Analysis and Interpretation 7
        Focus: Literary Elements (Point of View) 8
        Focus: Vocabulary Skills 9
    Chapters III–IV
        Reading Log 10
        Reading Check: Recalling the Facts 11
        Study Guide: Analysis and Interpretation 12
        Focus: Literary Elements (Characterization) 13
        Focus: Vocabulary Skills 14
    Chapter V
        Reading Log 15
        Reading Check: Recalling the Facts 16
        Study Guide: Analysis and Interpretation 17
        Focus: Literary Elements (Foreshadowing) 18
        Focus: Vocabulary Skills 19
    Chapters VI–VIII
        Reading Log 20
        Reading Check: Recalling the Facts 21
        Study Guide: Analysis and Interpretation 22
        Focus: Literary Elements (Symbolism) 23
        Focus: Vocabulary Skills 24
    Chapters IX–XII, Epilogue
        Reading Log 25
        Reading Check: Recalling the Facts 26
        Study Guide: Analysis and Interpretation 27
        Focus: Literary Elements (Situational Irony) 28
        Focus: Vocabulary Skills 29
Writing Assignment: Writing About Literature 30
Writing Assignment: Creative Writing 32
Projects 34
Suggested Readings 35

To the Student

This study guide contains materials that will help you to record your questions about and reactions to *The Time Machine* and to make notes as you read the novel. The study guide contains the following sections:

INTRODUCTION

This section provides you with background material important to an understanding of the novel. It acquaints you with the author's life, familiarizes you with the historical background of the book, and alerts you to some major characteristics of the novel.

CHAPTER CLUSTER WORKSHEETS

This section is the heart of the study guide. Some especially significant or complex chapters are treated singly, but more often the chapters are grouped or clustered. In each cluster there are five worksheets:

Reading Log. The log pages contain graphic organizers for keeping personal lists of quotations from the novel and asking questions you would like to have answered in class.

Reading Check: Recalling the Facts. This worksheet enables you to recall the *where*, *when*, *who*, and *what* of the chapter cluster. You will be able to find answers to the questions in the text of the novel. By successfully answering the Reading Check questions, you will be able to construct the plot summaries also called for on this worksheet.

Study Guide: Analysis and Interpretation. This worksheet contains questions that require you to go back into the chapters, to rethink what happens, what is said, and what meanings are emerging.

Focus: Literary Elements. This worksheet focuses on one of the literary characteristics significant to the chapter(s) reviewed in the worksheet—for example, symbolism.

Focus: Vocabulary Skills. This worksheet is designed to help you sharpen your vocabulary skills.

You might use the worksheets first as a prereading tool. Before reading a chapter or group of chapters, preview the appropriate cluster of worksheets. This will help you to focus your reading. Then, when you have read the designated section of the novel, complete the worksheets that your teacher has assigned. As you read succeeding chapters, you may find that you will add details to some of your earlier responses. Think of your completed worksheets as notes that you will use later to prepare for tests, to write papers, or to develop projects.

WRITING ASSIGNMENTS

Near the end of the study guide are two writing assignments: one analytical and one creative. These assignments will enrich your understanding of the novel.

PROJECTS

A list of projects has been provided. These projects will allow you to use special skills in the visual arts, photography, music, or drama, and will give you the opportunity to practice oral skills and research skills.

SUGGESTED READINGS

This is a list of additional works that you may wish to read.

Introduction to *The Time Machine*

Can you predict what life will be like 800,000 years from now? How might people have changed by then? Have you any ideas about what might happen in the far future in the very spot where you are sitting now?

Not just anyone can speculate intelligently about what might happen in the future. Those who can often possess three special gifts. First, they have an interest in science and technology. Second, they possess a vivid imagination. And third, they can look critically at their own time period.

A famous British author used all three of these special abilities to write some of the first science fiction novels. H. G. Wells was deeply interested in science and technology; he certainly had a vivid imagination; and he was an outspoken social critic of his time. Wells began his literary career in 1895 with the publication of *The Time Machine*. In this novel, a time traveler journeys 800,000 years into the future.

Historical Background

The nineteenth century was a time of rapid change, of important intellectual and scientific discoveries. In the midst of—and largely as a result of—this scientific revolution, another important revolution developed—the Industrial Revolution.

The Industrial Revolution

The term "Industrial Revolution" was originally used by an English historian to describe England's extraordinary economic development from 1760 to 1840. During this period, factories were built, new fuels and materials were developed, and significant advances were made in transportation and communication. Many scholars think that this revolution continued into the twentieth century.

Despite the many advantages of mass production, misery spread among factory workers in the great industrial cities of England. Until the end of the nineteenth century, workers (including small children) were often cruelly exploited. They worked for thirteen or more hours each day. Many children never saw daylight because they went to work before dawn and trudged home after dark. Mass unemployment became a common problem because newly created machines did the work of many people.

H.G. Wells was excited by the scientific advancements that made the Industrial Revolution possible, but he was deeply troubled by the resulting harmful side effects. His later novels reflect his opinion that science can produce sinister side effects unless it is monitored by responsible and compassionate people.

H. G. Wells

Born in 1866, Herbert George Wells was the third son of Sarah and Joseph Wells. He was born in a shabby little room over a china shop in Kent, England. This little boy, nicknamed Bertie, was to become a widely acclaimed novelist. As a child, however, Bertie felt the relentless pinch of poverty. His parents worked hard to provide food and shelter for their three sons, but they saw little reason to encourage the children to pursue a formal education. The two older boys seemed content to go into apprenticeships in their early teens. Young Bertie, however, was a voracious reader, and he seized every opportunity to educate himself.

A Fascination with Science

Sarah Wells took Bertie with her each day to the wealthy Sussex home of Sir Harry Featherstonhaugh, where she did domestic work. There the youngster discovered an enormous private library filled with exciting books by writers such as Jonathan Swift, Plato, and Voltaire. He read as many of these volumes as he could, and he remembered what he read. Young Wells was particularly fascinated by books that discussed scientific subjects.

At age fourteen, young Wells was apprenticed by his parents to a draper, a dealer in cloth and clothing, just as his two older brothers had been. He hated the grueling thirteen-hour-a-day job working for someone he thought to be both cruel and insensitive. During these years, Wells came to question a social system in which a person's life was rigidly determined by the social class of his or her parents.

Fortunately, Wells found an escape from the poverty into which he was born. In nineteenth-century England, nearly any young person could advance academically by passing the appropriate examinations along the way. It was not really necessary to attend classes to take these exams. Many wealthy students had private tutors; young Bertie Wells tutored himself. He began passing the examinations and displaying an unusual ability in science. At age eighteen, he received a scholarship from the Normal School of Science, South Kensington, to study to become a science teacher.

Darwin and Huxley's Influence on Wells

The publication of Charles Darwin's *On the Origin of Species by Means of Natural Selection* in 1859, seven years before Wells's birth, caused a great sensation. All 1,250 copies were sold out the first day. In this groundbreaking, controversial work, the result of careful, detailed study, Darwin presented his hypothesis that for millions of years all living creatures, including humans, had been gradually changing in form. Offspring always varied slightly from the parents. Eventually, those variations that helped a species to survive flourished, while those that were disabling gradually disappeared altogether. Darwin called nature's assistance in helping a species select and develop survival characteristics *natural selection*. The process of change and modification a species undergoes in order to survive he called *evolution*.

The theory of evolution through natural selection caused a deep, angry conflict between orthodox religion and science. Critics of the theory claimed that a belief in evolution—the gradual adaptation of plants and animals to their environment—left no place for divine guidance or design in the overall plan of life.

The rather shy, sensitive, and often sickly Darwin chose not to argue his theory publicly. Instead of taking part in often violent confrontations about his theory, he was content to let others defend it for him. One of Darwin's ardent defenders was the English biologist Thomas Henry Huxley. In addition to publicly championing his friend Darwin's views, Huxley also passed them along to his own biology students in South Kensington. One of these students was an intelligent and admiring young man named H. G. Wells.

As Huxley taught the young Wells and his peers the ideas and theories of Darwin, he convinced these impressionable students that the future could *only* be shaped by humanity's ethical control of the blind impulses of nature. Professor Huxley's greatest fear, it seemed, was that humans would eventually be powerless to control the evolutionary process. Not only was he doubtful that evolution would bring a better life on earth, but he implied that human beings could retrogress in their development—that is, become *worse*. He believed that the evolutionary process could destroy humankind altogether.

These suppositions must have provided H. G. Wells with many extraordinary possibilities as he asked himself questions that began with "What if . . . ?" His novels pose amazingly creative and gripping questions as well as the possible answers.

As an old man, Wells looked back on his year with Professor Huxley as the most exciting educational period of his life. He credited Charles Darwin and Thomas Henry Huxley with the nineteenth century's great intellectual revolution.

Wells the Writer

After his graduation from the University of London in 1888, H. G. Wells taught science for a brief time. Following a difficult period marked by ill health, financial complications, and an unhappy marriage, he began to write. His first published book was a biology textbook. Two years later, in 1895, he published *The Time Machine*, the first of his "scientific romances"— the precursors of science fiction. An immediate success, this novel was followed by *The Island of Dr. Moreau* (1896), *The Invisible Man* (1897), *The War of the Worlds* (1898), *The First Men in the Moon* (1901), and *The War in the Air* (1908).

Later, weary of these scientific romances, Wells began to write novels that expressed his hostility toward the rigid Victorian social order of the late nineteenth century. This trend led to his involvement in political journalism.

Wells was a prominent spokesman for the liberal, optimistic world view that prevailed before World War I. During this war, however, his faith in human progress was shaken. He proposed that people could make favorable progress only if they adapted themselves to changes of circumstances and environment. Wells believed that to adapt effectively, people must be well educated. Consequently, he set about writing his ambitious *Outline of History* (1920).

In later years, Wells urged an integrated global civilization. He was instrumental in creating what he called "a Universal Declaration of Human Rights." This document was the foundation for the declaration that was eventually adopted by the United Nations.

A Disillusioned Old Man

With the outbreak of World War II, Wells adopted a vision of a world in which nature destroys all humanity. In his last novel, *You Can't Be Too Careful* (1941), he describes humankind as blocking all paths toward the future. This stubborn, evil "mass" of humanity, as he describes it, cannot awaken to a world view or ethical "cosmopolis" that could save it from extinction.

Wells expressed his total despair in a thirty-seven-page pamphlet titled "Mind at the End of Its Tether." Published when he was seventy-nine, the pamphlet expresses Wells's deeply pessimistic view of a doomed universe devoid of recuperative power. H. G. Wells died in London in August 1946, a year after the atomic bomb was dropped over Hiroshima, Japan.

Literary Critics and H. G. Wells

During his lifetime, H. G. Wells was widely regarded as a brilliant man and a gifted writer. Writer and critic Henry James was somewhat more guarded. Although he thought Wells was surely gifted, he considered his fiction writing to be undisciplined and lacking in direction.

Actually, James and Wells disagreed about the purpose of fiction. While James thought "art" was the main purpose, Wells thought literature should convey a message. They debated the subject for fifteen years. Wells refused to back down from his position. All of Wells's scientific romances, including *The Time Machine*, have a moral, a message, or a warning.

For several decades following his death in 1946, critics largely ignored the writings of H. G. Wells. They loosely categorized his early novels with a new genre called "science fiction." In the second half of the twentieth century, however, Wells's writings have received renewed attention and interest.

Today, critics are concerned with H. G. Wells from two different perspectives. Some critics look at Wells as a sociological novelist. These critics point out Wells's concern with the values and organization of society and society's effect on human destiny. Those stories of Wells that reflect on political and social problems are compared to the writings of Wells's favorite writer, the eighteenth-century satirist Jonathan Swift.

Other critics emphasize Wells's role as a myth-maker. From the pages of Wells's books came extraordinary predictions of tanks, airplanes, aerial and atomic warfare, television, and brainwashing. He also provided us with vivid descriptions of assorted space creatures and evil scientists performing ghastly experiments. Wells's imagination produced striking archetypes that appear over and over in literature, film, and other media to the present day.

Major Characteristics

The Time Machine, like Wells's other scientific romances, contains grave warnings to a civilization exploring the vast possibilities of science and technology. However, *The Time Machine* is also an exciting adventure story that unravels the mysterious relationship between the innocent Eloi and the apelike Morlocks.

One of the major characteristics of Wells's novels is their meticulous attention to detail. Always a scientist as well as a writer, Wells probes characters and events as if they were being viewed on a microscope slide. To make the fantastic appear credible, he places humdrum, everyday details alongside the unbelievable. The Time Traveller is a cheerful, rather ordinary little man who takes tobacco for his pipe from a jar on the mantel. He performs this mundane task immediately after sending a model time machine into the fourth dimension.

A surprising characteristic of *The Time Machine* is Wells's use of vivid similes and metaphors, as well as strikingly poetic language. Near the end of the novel, there is a haunting description of a dying world. It is one of the most desolate images in all literature.

Finally, an important characteristic of *The Time Machine* is its powerful symbolism. Throughout this short novel, the thoughtful reader will sense the deeper meanings of darkness, machines, the underground, the Palace of Green Porcelain, and other elements of the story.

Although the characters created by H. G. Wells show little depth, the range of this author's imagination is impressive. His deliberate warning or message, his skillful use of detail, his poetic language, and his subtle use of symbolism all combine to produce a fascinating tale embedded with a somber warning.

Would you want to travel into the future if you were given the opportunity? What do you think you might find as you entered the world of A.D. 802,701?

NAME _____ CLASS _____ DATE _____

Reading Log

Chapters I–II

Questions for Class Discussion

Record at least one question that you would like to raise in class. Note your teacher's and your classmates' responses to your question or questions below.

Questions for Class Discussion	Answers Discussed in Class

Interpreting Quotations

Record one or two quotations that you find interesting or consider important. For example, you might choose a quotation because you agree or disagree with its idea; because you are puzzled by it; or because it helps you to understand some aspect of the content or style of the novel (such as theme, symbolism, or the use of figurative language). Note the page number where you found each quotation. Write some or all of the following comments: your interpretation, your teacher's comments, and the reaction of the class to each quotation.

Quotations	Page	Interpretations and Explanations

Novel Study Guide: *The Time Machine*

NAME _____ CLASS _____ DATE _____

Reading Check: Recalling the Facts

Chapters I–II

1. According to the Time Traveller, mathematicians believe that space has three dimensions. What are these three dimensions?

2. What fourth dimension interests the Time Traveller?

3. What does the Time Traveller say is the only difference between the fourth dimension and any of the three dimensions of space?

4. What do the two levers on the Time Machine model do?

5. What happens to the model of the Time Machine when the Psychologist presses the lever?

6. At the following Thursday's dinner, what message does the Time Traveller leave for the Medical Man?

7. Describe the Time Traveller's appearance when he arrives for the second dinner.

8. What food does the Time Traveller say it is a "treat" to eat again?

9. How long does the Time Traveller say he has lived since he left his laboratory on his journey?

10. About how long was the Time Traveller gone in relation to the clock in his laboratory?

Plot Summaries of Chapters I–II

Write a summary of each chapter, relating the major events. Include the setting and the main characters involved.

NAME _____ CLASS _____ DATE _____

Study Guide: Analysis and Interpretation

Chapters I–II

1. After the Time Traveller asserts that humans can move about in time much as they move about in space, Filby declares, "It's against reason." What does Filby mean by this statement?

2. How do the guests at the first dinner party seem to regard the Time Traveller?

3. Examine the last sentence in Chapter I. What does Filby's solemn wink reveal about him?

4. Why do you think the Time Traveller might have invited a Journalist and an Editor to the second dinner?

5. What do you think may have happened to alter so greatly the Time Traveller's appearance when he comes in late to the second dinner?

6. Is the narrator writing these two chapters before or after he has heard the Time Traveller's story? How do you know?

NAME _____ CLASS _____ DATE _____

Focus: Literary Elements

Chapters I–II

Point of View

Point of view is the vantage point or position from which a narrative is told. The two most frequently used points of view are **first-person** and **third-person**. In the first-person point of view, the story is narrated by one of the characters in his or her own words. The reader learns only what that character knows and sees. In the third-person point of view, the narrator, who is not a character in the story, may tell the story from the point of view of one particular character (third-person limited) or may be an all-knowing observer who can reveal what all the characters are thinking (third-person omniscient).

EXAMPLES:

First-Person Point of View: When I walked over to the wall separating the two rooms, I could hear soft, desperate whispers.

Third-Person Limited Point of View: Terry was savvy and streetwise. As she walked down the dimly lit sidewalk, she knew that someone could be waiting just around the corner.

Third-Person Omniscient Point of View. Philippe looked at Clara, and Clara looked at Philippe, and they both wondered how either could tolerate the other.

---

1. From which point of view are the first two chapters of *The Time Machine* told? How soon can you tell?

2. Although the narrator says that "Filby became pensive," why can't the narrator describe what Filby is thinking?

3. Place an *X* before the statement below that best illustrates the first-person point of view.
   a. _____ The Time Traveller smiled.
   b. _____ The Time Traveller was amused.
   c. _____ The Time Traveller was considering a sarcastic retort.

4. Explain why you rejected the other two choices above.

5. Why do you think a writer would deliberately limit the point of view in a story to include only what one character thinks, hears, and sees?

6. If a writer is telling a fantastic story as opposed to an ordinary, believable one, do you think that the use of first-person point of view would make the narrative more believable? Why or why not?

NAME _____ CLASS _____ DATE _____

Focus: Vocabulary Skills

Chapters I–II

An author who deals with the fantastic or the unbelievable tries to make his story seem *credible*, or believable, to the reader. In the opening chapters of *The Time Machine*, words that establish credibility are important. Read the following paragraph and notice how the italicized words are used. Then answer the questions that follow. Check your answers by consulting a dictionary.

> The Time Traveller tells his guests that it is possible to travel in time just as it is possible to travel in space. When his guests are *skeptical*, the Time Traveller says he has "experimental *verification*," and he brings in a small model of a time machine and makes it disappear. The Medical Man says that the idea of time travel sounds *plausible* at the moment but implies that it will seem otherwise in "the common sense of the morning." Then the Time Traveller leads his guests to the laboratory to show them the Time Machine in which he plans to travel. They follow him, "puzzled but *incredulous*." Afterwards, the narrator wonders about the *plausibility* of time travel.

1. Which word is nearest in meaning to *skeptical*?
   (a) amazing
   (b) doubtful
   (c) plausible

2. At the beginning of Chapter II, the narrator says that if Filby had shown the group the Time Machine and explained the subject just as the Time Traveller had done, they would have shown Filby "far less scepticism" (British spelling of *skepticism*). Which of the following statements is accurate?
   (a) They would have believed whatever Filby said.
   (b) They would have come closer to believing Filby than they did to believing the Time Traveller.
   (c) They would have believed Filby even less than they did the Time Traveller.

3. Which word or phrase is nearest in meaning to *plausible*?
   (a) unthinkable
   (b) obviously true
   (c) seemingly reasonable

4. Which word or phrase is nearest in meaning to *incredulous*?
   (a) withholding judgment
   (b) in suspense
   (c) unbelieving

5. Which word is nearest in meaning to *verification*?
   (a) proof
   (b) demonstration
   (c) reasons

NAME _____ CLASS _____ DATE _____

Reading Log

Chapters III–IV

Questions for Class Discussion

Record at least one question that you would like to raise in class. Note your teacher's and your classmates' responses to your question or questions below.

Questions for Class Discussion	Answers Discussed in Class

Interpreting Quotations

Record one or two quotations that you find interesting or consider important. For example, you might choose a quotation because you agree or disagree with its idea; because you are puzzled by it; or because it helps you to understand some aspect of the content or style of the novel (such as theme, symbolism, or the use of figurative language). Note the page number where you found each quotation. Write some or all of the following comments: your interpretation, your teacher's comments, and the reaction of the class to each quotation.

Quotations	Page	Interpretations and Explanations

NAME _____ CLASS _____ DATE _____

Reading Check: Recalling the Facts

Chapters III–IV

1. In his first quick experiment, the Time Traveller presses the stopping lever almost immediately. How far does he go into the future?

2. As the Time Traveller begins his real journey into the future, what is excessively painful to his eyes?

3. What tragic possibility does the Time Traveller say he once cheerfully accepted as an unavoidable risk in time travel?

4. What object does the Time Traveller see as the hail subsides?

5. What fears about future human beings does the Time Traveller harbor before he sees the frail people?

6. What does the Time Traveller do with the control levers to the Time Machine?

7. What year is it when the Time Traveller stops?

8. Briefly describe what the people look like.

9. What do these people eat?

10. According to the Time Traveller, if people subjugate nature, what will happen in the end?

Plot Summaries of Chapters III–IV

Write a summary of each chapter, relating the major events. Include the setting and the main characters involved.

HBJ material copyrighted under notice appearing earlier in this work.   Novel Study Guide: *The Time Machine* **11**

NAME _____ CLASS _____ DATE _____

Study Guide: Analysis and Interpretation

Chapters III–IV

1. Why does Mrs. Watchett appear to shoot across the room like a rocket?

2. As the Time Traveller moves in time, is he also moving in space? How do you know?

3. When the sky clears after the hailstorm, the Time Traveller is suddenly terrified. Why do you think he decides not to mount his machine and depart immediately?

4. What is the source of the Time Traveller's momentary "flow of disappointment"?

5. What makes the Time Traveller think that the socioeconomic system of this future culture is communism?

6. How does the Time Traveller explain his belief that he had traveled to a time when humanity was "on the wane"?

NAME _____ CLASS _____ DATE _____

Focus: Literary Elements

Chapters III–IV

Characterization

Characterization refers to the methods a writer uses to reveal a character's personality. A writer may reveal character by

1. giving a physical description of the character,
2. showing the character's actions,
3. revealing the character's words or thoughts,
4. having other characters express their opinions about the character, and/or
5. directly expressing his or her own opinions about the character.

The questions below provide practice in recognizing the methods of characterization.

1. Wells presents detailed descriptions of the beings the Time Traveller encounters in Chapters III and IV.
   a. How tall are these beings?
   b. What are they wearing?
   c. Describe their hair.
   d. What is distinctive about their mouths, ears, and eyes?

2. The author shows the characters in action.
   a. How do these future beings make certain that the Time Traveller is real?
   b. What do they put around his neck?
   c. One of the beings points to the sun and imitates the sound of thunder. What does this action seem to mean?

3. These future people speak in an unknown language. Wells describes the way their speech sounds to the Time Traveller.
   a. Give two details from the chapters that describe the people's speech.
   b. What does the people's speech indicate about their nature?

4. The Time Traveller, a character in the story, states his own opinions about the people of the future. List several of the opinions that he expresses.

5. Can you find examples of Wells directly expressing his own opinions about the character?

HBJ material copyrighted under notice appearing earlier in this work.   Novel Study Guide: *The Time Machine* 13

NAME _____ CLASS _____ DATE _____

Focus: Vocabulary Skills

Chapters III–IV

When readers find long or difficult words, they usually try to clarify meaning in one of three ways:

- They try to figure out meaning by studying the ideas around the word; these ideas or clues are called *context clues*.
- They find structural clues in the word itself, such as prefixes, suffixes, and roots.
- They look up the word in the dictionary and locate the particular definition that fits the meaning or context.

Notice the way the word *verdigris* is used in the following passage from Chapter III:

> "The pedestal, it appeared to me, was of bronze, and was thick with verdigris. . . . It was greatly weather-worn, and that imparted an unpleasant suggestion of disease."

- You might use the context to figure out the meaning of *verdigris*. You may know that bronze needs to be cleaned to stay shiny. Looking ahead in the paragraph, you can see that the pedestal has been neglected. If you have ever seen bronze that has not been cleaned for a while, you have seen verdigris.
- You might know that *verd* is a part of other words, like *verdant*, which means "green."
- You may use a dictionary to learn that *verdigris* is a green or bluish deposit of copper carbonates that forms on brass, copper, or bronze.

Use the three methods above to figure out the meaning of the word *hypertrophied* in the following passage from Chapter IV:

> ". . . innumerable tables made of slabs of polished stone, raised perhaps a foot from the floor, and upon these were heaps of fruits. Some I recognized as a kind of hypertrophied raspberry or orange, but for the most part they were strange."

1. What would you guess the word *hypertrophied* means, judging from the context clues? Write your guess, and then explain your reasoning.

2. Do you know the meaning of the prefix *hyper–*? List any other words you know that begin with this prefix. Try to write a definition of these words. Finally, write what you *think* is the meaning of *hypertrophied*.

3. Look up *hypertrophied* in the dictionary.
   a. Write the definition.
   b. Write the meaning of "hypertrophied raspberry or orange."

NAME _____ CLASS _____ DATE _____

Reading Log

Chapter V

Questions for Class Discussion

Record at least one question that you would like to raise in class. Note your teacher's and your classmates' responses to your question or questions below.

Questions for Class Discussion	Answers Discussed in Class

Interpreting Quotations

Record one or two quotations that you find interesting or consider important. For example, you might choose a quotation because you agree or disagree with its idea; because you are puzzled by it; or because it helps you to understand some aspect of the content or style of the novel (such as theme, symbolism, or the use of figurative language). Note the page number where you found each quotation. Write some or all of the following comments: your interpretation, your teacher's comments, and the reaction of the class to each quotation.

Quotations	Page	Interpretations and Explanations

HBJ material copyrighted under notice appearing earlier in this work.

Novel Study Guide: *The Time Machine*   **15**

NAME _____ CLASS _____ DATE _____

Reading Check: Recalling the Facts

Chapter V

1. What discovery does the Time Traveller make at the beginning of Chapter V?

2. Judging from the daylight behavior of the Eloi, the Time Traveller thinks they have forgotten fear. What shows him this assumption is not true?

3. Where does the Time Traveller decide the Time Machine is hidden?

4. What does the Time Traveller learn about the language of the childlike creatures?

5. What sound comes out of the circular wells?

6. How does Weena surprise the Time Traveller after he rescues her from drowning?

7. As dawn approaches, what does the Time Traveller fancy that he sees on a nearby hill?

8. As the Time Traveller reflects on his encounter with the little apelike creature in the gallery, what conclusion does he draw about the fate of the human species?

9. What are the Under-grounders called?

10. According to the Time Traveller's theory, the Upper-worlders, or Eloi, should be the masters. What signs of a lack of power puzzle the Time Traveller?

Plot Summary of Chapter V

Write a summary of the chapter, relating the major events. Include the setting and the main characters involved.

NAME _____ CLASS _____ DATE _____

Study Guide: Analysis and Interpretation

Chapter V

1. Why does the Time Traveller quickly dismiss the possibility that the little people have placed the Time Machine in some shelter for him?

2. How do you think the clothing and shoes of the Eloi are made?

3. Why do you think the other Eloi ignore the plight of the drowning girl?

4. Paraphrase the Time Traveller's theory about the future results of social differences between the Capitalist and the Labourer.

5. What do you infer about Weena in the last paragraph of Chapter V?

6. In this chapter, the Time Traveller begins to have almost a horror of the White Sphinx. He describes it as "white, shining, leprous, in the light of the rising moon"; it seems to smile at him mockingly. What might be the significance of the whiteness of the sphinx?

NAME _____ CLASS _____ DATE _____

Focus: Literary Elements

Chapter V

Foreshadowing

Foreshadowing refers to the clues a writer provides to suggest to the reader what may happen later. The use of foreshadowing builds suspense and helps to sustain the reader's interest.

In Chapter III, just after the Time Traveller lands in the future world, some frightening questions occur to him: "What might not have happened to men? What if cruelty had grown into a common passion? What if in this interval the race had lost its manliness, and had developed into something inhuman, unsympathetic, and overwhelmingly powerful?"

When the Time Traveller meets the frail people, he forgets these dark thoughts. In Chapter V, however, he learns that there are underground dwellers, and he senses again the presence of "something inhuman, unsympathetic, and overwhelmingly powerful." The reader may already suspect that the Time Traveller's original questions foreshadow some of the discoveries he will make about what has happened to human beings.

1. At the end of Chapter IV, the Time Traveller speculates that the innocent creatures have become weak because struggles or problems no longer exist. Then he adds, "Very simple was my explanation, and plausible enough—as most wrong theories are!" What might this statement foreshadow?

2. When the Time Traveller dismisses the possibility that the Eloi have taken the Time Machine, he is suddenly dismayed. What foreshadowing thoughts come to him?

3. As the Time Traveller gropes among the moonlit ruins, despairing over his missing machine, he touches "strange creatures in the black shadows." What discovery by the Time Traveller does this foreshadow?

4. What is foreshadowed by the wells and the sounds that come from them?

5. One night, the Time Traveller thinks he sees some white apelike figures carrying a dark body. What might this foreshadow?

NAME _____ CLASS _____ DATE _____

Focus: Vocabulary Skills

Chapter V

Certain specialized words are commonly used to describe human language. The Time Traveller uses several of these words to describe the language of the Eloi: "Either I missed some subtle point, or their language was excessively simple—almost exclusively composed of concrete substantives and verbs. There seemed to be few, if any, abstract terms, or little use of figurative language." Use a dictionary to help you answer the following questions about the passage.

1a. What is a *substantive*?
 b. Give an example of a childlike sentence in which, simply, a substantive is followed by a verb.

2a. What is the meaning of the adjective *abstract*?
 b. The opposite of the adjective *abstract* is the adjective *concrete*. What does *concrete* mean, as it relates to words and language?
 c. Identify each of the following words as *abstract* or *concrete*.
    (1) ambition
    (2) sacrifice
    (3) Weena
    (4) pedestal
    (5) courage

3. One definition of *figurative language* is "language that expresses one thing in terms of another." Figurative language often suggests the likeness of one thing to another. The phrase "ape-like creature," for example, compares the creature to an ape; it does not say that the creature *is* an ape.

 Identify the figurative language in each of the following quotations from Chapter V and explain what two things are being compared in each example.
 (a) " 'At once, like a lash across the face, came the possibility of losing my own age....' "
 (b) " 'But in all of them I heard a certain sound; a thud–thud–thud, like the beating of some big engine....' "
 (c) " 'I felt hopelessly cut off from my own kind—a strange animal in an unknown world.' "
 (d) " 'It was a foolish impulse, but the devil begotten of fear and blind anger was ill curbed and still eager to take advantage of my perplexity.' "

NAME _____ CLASS _____ DATE _____

Reading Log

Chapters VI–VIII

Questions for Class Discussion

Record at least one question that you would like to raise in class. Note your teacher's and your classmates' responses to your question or questions below.

Questions for Class Discussion	Answers Discussed in Class

Interpreting Quotations

Record one or two quotations that you find interesting or consider important. For example, you might choose a quotation because you agree or disagree with its idea; because you are puzzled by it; or because it helps you to understand some aspect of the content or style of the novel (such as theme, symbolism, or the use of figurative language). Note the page number where you found each quotation. Write some or all of the following comments: your interpretation, your teacher's comments, and the reaction of the class to each quotation.

Quotations	Page	Interpretations and Explanations

NAME _____ CLASS _____ DATE _____

Reading Check: Recalling the Facts

Chapters VI–VIII

1. The Time Traveller says that perhaps his restlessness and insecurity were the cause of his expedition southwestward. While on this expedition, what ruin does he see in the distance?

2. What does the Time Traveller hear as he descends into the well?

3. What does the Time Traveller smell as he enters the arched cavern of the Morlocks?

4. What does the Time Traveller wonder about as he views the Morlocks' table?

5. The Time Traveller regrets not having brought weapons, tobacco, medicine, and a camera. Why did he not come better equipped for his experience in a future world?

6. How does the Time Traveller happen to have the white flowers in his pocket?

7. What is the Time Traveller's plan for Weena's future?

8. What was the large porcelain building used for in earlier years?

9. If they had not been dummies, how was the Time Traveller going to use the dynamite cartridges?

10. What three things does the Time Traveller find useful for his purposes in the Palace of Green Porcelain?

Plot Summaries of Chapters VI–VIII

Write a summary of each chapter, relating the major events. Include the setting and the main characters involved.

NAME _____ CLASS _____ DATE _____

Study Guide: Analysis and Interpretation

Chapters VI–VIII

1. Why do you think the Morlocks clutch and pull at the Time Traveller?

2. Do you think the Time Traveller could have escaped the Morlocks without the four matches? Explain your answer.

3. In these chapters, the Time Traveller is preoccupied with his feelings toward the Morlocks. How do his descriptions of the Morlocks reveal his feelings? In your answer, give examples of descriptive details that appeal to the senses of sight, sound, touch, and smell. (See especially Chapter VI.)

4. What second hypothesis about the relationship between the Eloi and the Morlocks does the Time Traveller decide is wrong? With what new hypothesis does he replace it?

5. At the end of Chapter VII, the Time Traveller blames human selfishness for the evolution of the human race into the Eloi and the Morlocks. Why might this idea help the Time Traveller to push back his growing sense of horror? Explain whether or not he succeeds in doing so.

NAME _____ CLASS _____ DATE _____

Focus: Literary Elements

Chapters VI–VIII

Symbolism

A **symbol** is an object, person, place, or action that has meaning in itself and that also stands for something larger than itself. Symbols can also have multiple meanings. For example, in *The Time Machine*, the machine itself is a mechanism for travel in the fourth dimension. For the Time Traveller, however, the machine comes to stand for something more than just a machine; it is a symbol of scientific and technological progress, a marvel enabling humankind to discover exciting truths about the future.

H. G. Wells's *The Time Machine* contains other symbols. The following questions will help you identify some of them.

1. The Morlocks are small apelike creatures that live underground. For the Time Traveller, they become symbols of something more. Reread the first paragraph of Chapter VII. What do you think the Morlocks symbolize?

2. For the Time Traveller, the tall pinnacles of the Palace of Green Porcelain and the polished gleam of its walls seem symbolic. That is, they seem to stand for something more than just a structure. Explain this symbolism.

3. The two little white flowers that Weena places in the Time Traveller's pocket seem to take on a special meaning. Explain how these flowers could be interpreted symbolically.

4. The Time Traveller wishes he had a battering ram to break down the doors of the pedestal of the winged sphinx. What meanings do this statue and pedestal suggest? (You might consider the meaning of the word *sphinx*, the history and condition of the statue, the outspread wings, and the hollowness of the pedestal.)

5. When the Time Traveller descends into the subterranean world of the Morlocks, great shapes that look like big machines seem to rise out of the dim light and cast grotesque black shadows in which the Morlocks find shelter from the light. This description implies that these machines are a symbol of what?

6. Nearly everything in this future world is symbolic to the Time Traveller as he searches for the meaning of what he sees. What does this symbolism add to the story? Consider both the symbolic meanings and the effect of the use of symbolism on your response to the story.

NAME _____ CLASS _____ DATE _____

Focus: Vocabulary Skills

Chapters VI–VIII

A. Many words in *The Time Machine* are selected to create an atmosphere of decay and evil.

Match each numbered word below with the letter of the correct definition. You may use a dictionary to determine meanings if you wish.

_____ 1. vermin   a. state of decline; moral or intellectual decadence

_____ 2. malignant   b. evil in nature, influence, or effect

_____ 3. nemesis   c. made thoroughly dry; dried out

_____ 4. loathe   d. to detest, dislike greatly; view with disgust

_____ 5. degradation   e. small harmful or annoying insects or animals that are hard to control

_____ 6. deliquesced   f. uselessness

_____ 7. desiccated   g. a powerful, usually vicious opponent

_____ 8. futility   h. became soft or liquid with age

B. Provide the missing words in each of the following sentences from *The Time Machine*. Use the words listed in Part A above. Write out each word.

1. "A few shrivelled and blackened vestiges of what had once been stuffed animals, _____ mummies in jars that had once held spirit, a brown dust of departed plants: that was all!" (Chapter VIII)

2. "But, clearly, the old order was already in part reversed. The _____ of the delicate ones was creeping on apace." (Chapter VII)

3. ". . . but there was an altogether new element in the sickening quality of the Morlocks— a something inhuman and _____." (Chapter VII)

4. "But I could find no saltpeter; indeed, no nitrates of any kind. Doubtless they had _____ ages ago." (Chapter VIII)

5. "However great their intellectual _____, the Eloi had kept too much of the human form not to claim my sympathy. . . ." (Chapter VII)

24 Novel Study Guide: *The Time Machine*

NAME _____ CLASS _____ DATE _____

Reading Log

Chapters IX–XII, Epilogue

Questions for Class Discussion

Record at least one question that you would like to raise in class. Note your teacher's and your classmates' responses to your question or questions below.

Questions for Class Discussion	Answers Discussed in Class

Interpreting Quotations

Record one or two quotations that you find interesting or consider important. For example, you might choose a quotation because you agree or disagree with its idea; because you are puzzled by it; or because it helps you to understand some aspect of the content or style of the novel (such as theme, symbolism, or the use of figurative language). Note the page number where you found each quotation. Write some or all of the following comments: your interpretation, your teacher's comments, and the reaction of the class to each quotation.

Quotations	Page	Interpretations and Explanations

NAME _____ CLASS _____ DATE _____

Reading Check: Recalling the Facts

Chapters IX–XII, Epilogue

1. The Time Traveller and Weena leave the Palace of Green Porcelain late in the afternoon. What is the Time Traveller's plan for the night?

2. When the Time Traveller says, "I felt as if I was in a monstrous spider's web," to what is he referring?

3. What discovery does the Time Traveller make when he returns to the White Sphinx?

4. What have the Morlocks done to the machine they hid in the pedestal?

5. When the Time Traveller is finally able to escape, where does he go?

6. What kinds of creatures does the Time Traveller see on his journey following his escape from the world of the Eloi and the Morlocks?

7. When he returns to the present time, why does the Time Traveller land in a different corner of his laboratory?

8. Who returns to talk further with the Time Traveller?

9. How long does the narrator say the Time Traveller has been gone on this last journey?

10. What do the white flowers represent for the narrator?

Plot Summaries of Chapters IX–XII, Epilogue

Write a summary of each chapter, relating the major events. Include the setting and the main characters involved.

NAME _____ CLASS _____ DATE _____

Study Guide: Analysis and Interpretation

Chapters IX–XII, Epilogue

1. How well did the Time Traveller plan his trip to and from the Palace of Green Porcelain? Do you think that if he had planned differently, Weena might not have lost her life? Explain your answer.

2. The Time Traveller was glad to find three things in the Palace of Green Porcelain that he thought would help him to recover the Time Machine. Explain how each of the three—the camphor, the matches, and the iron bar—does or does not help in the recovery of the machine.

3. Why do you think the Time Traveller's guests do not take his story seriously? Does their attitude affect your feelings toward the Time Traveller? Explain.

4. In Chapter XII, why is the Time Traveller making another journey, and how might the camera and knapsack relate to his purpose?

5. Why do you think the narrator has chosen to tell the Time Traveller's story?

6. Examine the Time Traveller's thoughts in Chapter X. What messages do you think Wells wants to convey to readers of *The Time Machine*?

NAME _____ CLASS _____ DATE _____

Focus: Literary Elements

Chapters IX–XII, Epilogue

Situational Irony

Situational irony is a contrast between what is expected to happen and what actually happens. Here is an example of situational irony: A friend works hard to persuade you to go to see a movie that you feel certain will be extremely boring. Finally, but reluctantly, you agree to go. It turns out that the movie is the best one you've seen in a long time, while your friend is so bored by it that he almost goes to sleep in the theater.

A. Each of the following incidents is found in Chapters IX–XII of *The Time Machine*. Complete each sentence with a statement showing the situational irony of the incident.

1. Although the Time Traveller has matches, when he enters the pedestal, _____ _____.

2. Despite the Time Traveller's desire to protect Weena at all costs, _____ _____.

3. The morning after the fire, the Time Traveller approaches the pedestal, ready to assault it with his crowbar, but _____ _____ _____.

4. The Time Traveller at first assumes that the open doors of the pedestal mean that the Morlocks are meekly surrendering the Time Machine; however, _____ _____.

5. The Time Traveller, on his last journey, takes with him a camera and a knapsack, but _____ _____ _____.

B. Many of the Time Traveller's first expectations and perceptions of the future world turn out to be ironic. He soon learns that things are not what they seem. Look back at Chapters III–VIII of the novel and find two other examples of situational irony.

28 Novel Study Guide: *The Time Machine* HBJ material copyrighted under notice appearing earlier in this work.

NAME _____ CLASS _____ DATE _____

Focus: Vocabulary Skills

Chapters IX–XII, Epilogue

H. G. Wells was an excellent biology student before he became a writer. This may be why *The Time Machine* contains many exact descriptions of various creatures. These descriptions include vivid words that appeal to the reader's senses as well as to the imagination.

1. In Chapter IX, the eyes of the Morlocks are described by the Time Traveller as shining "like carbuncles."
   a. What is a *carbuncle*?
   b. What feeling do you get about an eye that looks like a carbuncle?

2. In the description of the monster crabs in Chapter XI, one crab's antennae are compared to "carters' whips, waving and feeling."
   a. What is a *carter*?
   b. What impression of the crab does this description give you?

3. The crab's back is "corrugated and ornamented with ungainly bosses" and blotched with a greenish "incrustation." The Time Traveller sees "the many palps of its complicated mouth."
   a. What is the texture or feeling of something that is *corrugated*?
   b. Define the word *ungainly*.
   c. What is the meaning of *bosses* in this context?
   d. Define *incrustation*.
   e. What is a *palp*?

4. The claws of the monster crab that the Time Traveller discovers behind him are "smeared with an algal slime."
   a. What is the noun plural form of *algal*?
   b. What texture does slime have?

Writing Assignment: Writing About Literature

ASSIGNMENT

Compare and contrast the Eloi and the Morlocks with respect to the human qualities they retain.

Here are some suggestions that you can use for planning, writing, and evaluating and revising your paper. Depending on your teacher's directions, you may follow some or all of these suggestions, or you may explore the subject in another way.

Prewriting

Step 1
Throughout his story, the Time Traveller describes and analyzes the Eloi and the Morlocks according to how human or inhuman they seem to him. Looking back through the novel, make a list of specific characteristics of the Eloi and a list of specific characteristics of the Morlocks. The Time Traveller tells what the people of the future are like by describing their appearance, their speech, and their lifestyle; by giving examples of their actions; by analyzing and explaining their characteristics; and by presenting his feelings toward them. In addition, he reveals much about the Eloi through his depiction of Weena.

Include in your notes any quotations from the novel that might be especially helpful in supporting your characterization of the Eloi and the Morlocks.

Step 2
Both the Eloi and the Morlocks are descended from human beings. As they developed in opposite directions, both lost many human qualities. Three examples of human qualities are intelligence, imagination, and altruism. List several other examples of mental and emotional qualities that can be considered human. Then tell whether, in your opinion, each quality is evident to any extent in the Eloi and the Morlocks. You might put your ideas in a chart like the following.

Human Quality	Eloi	Morlocks
Intelligence	Very little—level of five-year-olds	Some—needed to run machinery
Imagination		
Altruism		

Step 3
Sketch out a plan for your paper. A comparison/contrast paper may point out both similarities and differences, but it should emphasize one or the other. You might first point out the similarities between the two groups, since both are lacking in human qualities, then focus on the

continued ☞

30   Novel Study Guide: *The Time Machine*   HBJ material copyrighted under notice appearing earlier in this work.

differences in the body of your paper. For this topic, the clearest organizational pattern would be to present all your points about one group and then all your points about the other group. You might have two paragraphs in the body of your essay, one on each group. In concluding, you might relate your comparison to Wells's theme or message.

Think through or jot down your answers to the following questions before you begin writing:
(a) What similarities do you see between the Eloi and the Morlocks?
(b) What are the main differences?
(c) Are the differences in the human qualities of the two groups really as great as they seem to the Time Traveller?
(d) What message does Wells convey to you about human progress or about what it means to be human?

Writing

1. In your introductory paragraph, give enough background information about the story to interest someone who has not read it. Next, you might explain the similarities between the Eloi and the Morlocks. You might end your introductory paragraph with a thesis statement that emphasizes the differences between the Eloi and the Morlocks or draws a conclusion about the degree to which the two groups retain human qualities.

2. Follow the same basic pattern in each body paragraph. Begin with a topic sentence about the human or inhuman qualities of the Eloi or the Morlocks. Then discuss the characteristics of the group, giving details that you listed in Prewriting Steps 1 and 2. You might focus directly on the human characteristics that you listed in Step 2, discussing them in the same order for each group. Or you might focus on the Time Traveller's response to the two groups. Be sure to use the same approach in each paragraph and to make the contrast clear.

3. Your concluding paragraph might make a statement about what it means to be human, why human qualities are valuable, or about what forces can contribute to making people less than human.

Evaluating, Revising, and Proofreading

Reread your essay with your audience in mind. Could someone who has not read the novel understand your essay? Could someone who has read the novel learn something or get a new insight from your essay?

Check to see whether you have used the same basic pattern for the two body paragraphs and whether you have included clear transitions between the paragraphs.

Examine your language. Is it as specific as possible? Have you used a variety of verbs? Have you given your reader a vivid picture of the future people?

You may find that you need more supporting evidence from the novel to support your position. If so, compile additional examples and quotations that you can incorporate as you revise. Check to see that you have used quotation marks accurately and that you have worked quotations from the novel smoothly into your own sentence structure. Finally, review your essay to locate and correct errors in grammar, usage, and mechanics.

Writing Assignment: Creative Writing

ASSIGNMENT

Where would you most like to go if you could make a journey in time? Explain the reasons for your choice, describe your preparations for your journey, and tell what you might expect to find at your destination.

Following are some suggestions for planning, writing, and evaluating and revising your paper. Depending on your teacher's directions, you may follow some or all of these suggestions, or you may explore the subject in another way.

Prewriting

Step 1
First, decide where you would like to go on your journey. Would you like to go into the past? If so, to what time period? Would you like to go into the future? If so, how far? Give the reasons for your choice. What would you like to learn, explore, or experience? Take the time to browse through history books, novels, magazines, and encyclopedias as you explore these questions.

Step 2
Decide what you would want to take with you on your journey, and make a packing list. What clothing and personal supplies might you need? Is there anything you might want to use to impress the people you visit? What could you use for bringing back souvenirs?

Step 3
Consider what you might find when you reach your destination. Although you do not know what you will find, you have probably based your preparations on some concrete expectation. What dangers should you be prepared for? How do you think you might communicate with the people? How will nature and technology be different from the way they are now? What would you *like* to find? What do you hope *not* to find?

Writing

1. Choose one of the following approaches:
   - Imagine where you would like to go even though you know it is impossible.
   - Imagine that you are actually going someday.
   - Tell in narrative form the story of your preparations, explaining how you happen to be going on a journey in time, describing your time machine, and so forth.

2. You should be able to develop a paragraph around your answers to the Prewriting questions in each of the three steps above. However, if you find you have more to say in response to the questions in Step 1, for example, you might develop two paragraphs around that step and perhaps combine in one paragraph your responses from Steps 2 and 3.

continued

Evaluating, Revising, and Proofreading

Make sure you have written your paper as clearly as possible. Have you explained your reasons carefully? Have you included specific details? Do your sentences follow each other smoothly and clearly?

Think about how interesting your classmates would find what you have written. Add at least one unusual or surprising detail to your paper, and give the paper a catchy title. Make any necessary revisions, and locate and correct errors in grammar, usage, and mechanics. When you have finished your paper, share it with your classmates.

Projects

1. Create a model of the Time Traveller's Time Machine, or design a Time Machine of your own.

2. Illustrate in some form the difference between the Eloi and the Morlocks. You might draw side-by-side pictures of an Eloi and a Morlock, or you might draw a diagram showing the Upper-world on top and the Under-world below.

3. Draw or paint a picture of the landscape based on a description from the novel. This might be a landscape from the world of the Eloi or one from the more distant future to which the Time Traveller journeys before he returns to the present.

4. Plan and execute a series of small pencil or ink drawings for *The Time Machine*, one to be placed at the beginning of each chapter. These can be very simple. Explain why you think each of your designs is appropriate for that chapter.

5. Suppose that the Journalist had believed the Time Traveller's story. Write the article that might have appeared in the newspaper the next day. Be sure to include a headline.

6. Research the early history of science fiction literature, and report to the class on Wells's role in the development of science fiction.

7. Research the Egyptian statue of the Sphinx and the Greek myth of the Sphinx. Report to the class or write a short paper on the relevance of any of your findings to the sphinxlike statue in the novel.

8. Stage a dramatic presentation of a scene from *The Time Machine*.

Suggested Readings

Auel, Jean
   Clan of the Cave Bear
Boulle, Pierre
   Planet of the Apes
Huxley, Aldous
   Brave New World
L'Engle, Madeleine
   A Wrinkle in Time
Orwell, George
   1984
Verne, Jules
   A Journey to the Center of the Earth
   The Mysterious Island
   Twenty Thousand Leagues Under the Sea

Wells, H. G.
  Fiction
     The Wonderful Visit
     The Island of Doctor Moreau
     The Invisible Man
     The War of the Worlds
     The First Men in the Moon
     In the Days of the Comet
     The History of Mr. Polly
     Mr. Brittling Sees It Through
     Tono-Bungay
     The Shape of Things to Come
     Kipps
     The New Machiavelli
  Nonfiction
     The Work, Wealth, and Happiness of Mankind
     The Outline of History
     The Science of Life
     Experiment in Autobiography

NOTES

NOTES

NOTES

NOTES

NOTES

NOTES

NOTES